SPIRAL

THE JOURNEY HOME

BY

T. L. CONN

For my Daughter, Deanna, & Girls.

Special thanks to my niece, Melissa, for her gracious support & expertise.

TABLE OF CONTENTS

Chapter 1 1

Chapter 2 12

Chapter 3 24

Chapter 4 35

Chapter 5 46

Chapter 6 59

Chapter 7 69

Chapter 8 80

CHAPTER 1

The hour was late. Fatigue gnawed at the shoulders of the hopeful who had waited endless hours and days for word of recovery, faith alone, lifting belief that all would be well again.

The waiting room at St. Joseph Memorial Hospital was nearly empty now. Only the low, monotonous sound of the TV news commentator periodically broke the silence. The Covid 19 Pandemic had just claimed one million American souls. Variants and mutations were still surging, assuring that number would rise. Even so, true heroism prevailed as medical staff across the country gave their all to save as many as they could. Tonight, a miraculous recovery was underway.

33-year-old, Kathryn Peters, was finally coming out of a medically induced coma. It was a Hail Mary measure to save her life as she had been induced and placed on a ventilator for 42 days during her life-and-death struggle.

The inner door opened, and a nurse stepped into the waiting room. She quietly approached Kathryn's sister, Jackie, and sat down next to her.

"She's doing well. It will be some time until she is fully awake, but her lungs are taking oxygen, and her blood count has greatly improved. She's going to make it. Go home and rest now."

As Kathryn began to wake, her body felt like lead. It was difficult to move about, her throat felt scratchy, and her back was stiff and sore. Confused, she slowly brought her hand to her chest and stared at the ceiling. Where was she? What had happened to her?

Nightmarish visions still filled her mind of strange people and frightening events. She wanted to return to reality but was unable to discern which path to take. Flashbacks were swirling within her consciousness in a continual loop. She closed her eyes and concentrated on every breath.

When she again opened her eyes, she searched the room for clues. Yet nothing in her surroundings was familiar. Even those with her were unrecognizable as masks, and protective clothing covered their bodies.

"Welcome back, Kathryn. You've been asleep for a long time," said the nurse.

"Asleep?" questioned Kathryn.

"Yes, a long time," added the nurse. "We're taking good care of you. Dr. Fridrich is on his way."

The nurse hovered around her, making her comfortable and warm.

Kathryn's mind drifted in and out of fogginess for several minutes as she tried to focus more clearly. She noticed a white clock on the wall and wondered if it was day or night.

"Dr. Fridrich is here now, Kathryn."

The nurse stepped aside, allowing the doctor to stand next to her.

When she turned toward him, she saw a tall man dressed in scrubs. Instantly, she felt a jolt of shock. His eyes were terrifying, and his body appeared to morph into two different identities, shifting back and forth yet somehow staying the same. She recoiled, filled with horror, and clenched her fists. Desperately, she tried to push away from him but felt frozen in place, too weak to move. Then, reality spiraled out of control, forcing her mind into another temporal dimension.

"You will tell us what we want to know, Fraulein. We do not wish to harm you further."

Kathryn was seated in a chair across from a uniformed German Commandant. Two SS guards stood on either side of her. She sensed she'd seen the Commandant somewhere before, there was something about his eyes that seemed familiar.

Was this 1945 Nazi Germany? Was she being interrogated? If so, how and for what? She responded to his threats, surprised by her own German accent.

"I do not know what it is you want from me," she answered.

Her body ached from numerous blows, and the straps binding her to the chair cut deep into her swollen wrists. How was this possible? She couldn't make sense of her predicament. Was it World War II? Did they think she was a spy or with the resistance?

"Where are your comrades hiding? Tell us where they are," the Commandant demanded.

"I do not know, sir. I do not know."

"Again."

Immediately, one of the guards struck her, and she reeled with the pain. The Commandant rose from his chair and approached her, leaning inches away from her face, menacing and dangerous.

"We have many methods to get what we want, Fraulein. It would be a shame to destroy such a pretty face. You would be wise to save yourself."

Breathless, Kathryn responded, a tear rolling down her cheek.

"I do not wish to be here, sir. But how can I tell you what I do not know?"

His face tightened into an ugly scowl, and he turned away from her. Walking back to his desk, his stomach growled loudly. He shook his head.

"It is late. Take her back to her cell to reconsider her obstinacy. We will continue tomorrow. I am hungry now."

The guards released her from the chair and dragged her away from the interrogation room. She made no sound. The Commandant dropped heavily into his seat and poured a glass of Cognac.

The long, darkened corridors of the confiscated German castle were cold and damp but welcome nonetheless. At least she was out of the chair. As they rounded a corner, one of the guards suddenly dropped to the floor. A struggle ensued. The second guard was overtaken by the men waiting in the darkness and quickly silenced.

"Elsa, come with me. We're getting you out of here," a husky voice whispered in her ear.

She was quickly wrapped in a warm blanket and hurried through the corridors. Gratefully surprised, she caught a glimpse of the handsome face of her rescuer. She knew that face, and her heart soared. She was safe now.

"Doctor, what is happening to her? Is she relapsing into a coma?"

The nurse couldn't believe her eyes. Kathryn's condition was unexpected and concerning. No other Covid patient had exhibited this strange behavior.

Dr. Fridrich checked her vital signs. She was breathing on her own, but her blood pressure was much higher than before. Kathryn seemed to be trapped in some kind of dream, a neurological phenomenon of distorted reality. He'd studied recent medical journals describing unusual aftereffects while a patient exited a coma. Every patient tolerated the experience differently, yet thankfully, none were life-threatening.

"No. We need to give her more time. She'll come around when she's ready. Keep her comfortable and continue intravenous fluids. She's strong, and she's young."

Elsa was taken to a secure location and given food and water. Her rescuer cradled her in his arms and tenderly wiped away the blood that had marked her beautiful face. She instinctively knew he was someone she loved.

"Thank you. Thank you," she said softly.

"Hans, we need to prepare for tomorrow." The men were waiting for him to join them.

"Ja, tomorrow," agreed Hans.

He laid her down on a cot and covered her with the blanket.

"Elsa, I am right here," he assured her, stroking her long dark hair. "Rest now."

Hans joined the other men at the makeshift table, where a single lantern illuminated a map that lay on the surface. They spoke in low tones while studying the map.

The Germans had stockpiled munitions at several locations in Berlin. They were heavily guarded.

But one of those locations, a warehouse along the river, was only guarded on three sides, as the rear exterior was partially submerged. The plan was to create diversions before dawn at both ends of the building, drawing the guards toward the chaos. They would then enter the building from the riverside and plant timed charges that would set off a chain reaction inside. It would be a costly blow to the Third Reich.

The men rested before it was time to leave. Some tried to read, some slept, some prayed.

Hans joined Elsa on the cot and lay next to her. They held each other in a long embrace, gently caressing one another until they drifted into sleep together.

Too few hours passed before the men began to stir. They checked and readied their weapons, strapping on side arms and packed the explosive devices needed to carry out their raid.

Hans kissed Elsa and rose from the cot.

"It is time, Elsa. I must go now," said Hans.

"I'm coming with you. Don't leave me here alone." she insisted.

Hans shook his head. "No, Elsa. It's not safe."

One of the men interrupted, "If she wants to come, let her. The SS might discover this place before we return."

Elsa and Hans longingly looked into each other's eyes. With great reservation, Hans silently nodded.

"You will stay in the boat."

"I will," she agreed.

When they were ready, they exited the building in the pre-dawn darkness one by one, careful to stagger their egress minutes apart. Those responsible for creating the diversions went on ahead. Hans, Elsa, and two others went to the boat dock.

The streets were empty. The early morning chill filled the air, and the river Spree was flat- calm. The men took great care to row without making ripples or splashing sounds. Elsa sat closely with Hans, her heart pounding in anticipation of the mission ahead. She looked at the stars and wondered why she was there. Nothing seemed real or even possible. Yet, here she was.

When they reached the warehouse, they quietly lowered the anchor and held position next to the exterior of the brick building.

Hans checked his watch.

"Soon now."

The men readied their explosive devices and positioned themselves for entry through a window above them.

Then, all hell broke loose.

Simultaneous explosions occurred at each end of the building. Shouting and gunfire immediately ensued as the guards fought their attackers. More explosions shattered the once peaceful night, and screams of the wounded and dying intermittently accompanied the reverberation.

Hans and his men quickly scaled the wall and broke into the window. They had a precise time limit to get in, set the charges, and get out before the diversions ended.

Elsa waited for their return. She was terribly frightened and worried about their safety. But within minutes, the men exited the window and repelled down the brick wall, again joining her in the boat. They raised anchor and pushed away from the warehouse, rowing quickly to get to a safe distance before the charges went off.

When the skirmish with the guards subsided, it became briefly still. The acrid smell of gunpowder filled the air.

Within minutes, the boat was safely downstream before multiple explosions pierced the silence. The sounds were horrendous.

They had successfully set off the chain reaction they had meticulously planned. The windows of the warehouse were blown out and chunks of brick rained down into the river. The munitions inside exploded with an endless domino effect. The building was taken apart piece by piece.

They had, indeed, dealt heavy damage to Hitler's war effort. Even so, the men knew his revenge would be swift and brutal.

CHAPTER 2

At sunrise, the men discarded the boat and separated. They would meet again at a prearranged location. By now, the Gestapo were everywhere. They raced through the streets of Berlin, questioning everyone they encountered like a swarm of hungry insects.

When Hans and Elsa reached the safe house, they found it heavily guarded. Hans knew it meant the SS had captured one or more of the men during the raid, and its location had been compromised.

They had to find a way out of the city. They walked away, arm and arm like lovers, and went to a bridge over the river Spree.

Stopping midway, Hans held Elsa closely and whispered, "Come away with me. We can go to Holland, become man and wife, and live in peace."

Elsa backed away in confusion.

"But I can't, Hans. This is all wrong," she said.

"Yes, yes, you can. I will take care of you," he implored.

"I am so sorry, please forgive me. I don't know how to explain it, but I'm not supposed to be here."

Hans took her face in his hands.

"Trust me, Elsa."

Suddenly, they heard loud whistles and shouting. SS guards were approaching them from both sides of the bridge. Sadly, one of the captured comrades pointed them out. He had been badly tortured and was being propped up by two guards.

"Elsa, you must go!" said Hans looking over the railing of the bridge.

"Where?"

"Into the water, now!" he said, lifting her over the railing and gave her a push.

Shots rang out on the bridge just as she hit the water.

Within seconds, there were bullets zinging in the water all around her, and she quickly dove deeper. She swam away from the bridge as far as she could before being forced to surface for air. When she finally did, she instantly became confused and disoriented.

The water felt and smelled completely different. It was much colder, and it was salty. This was not a river at all. She was in an ocean.

She heard terrible screams and the deep groaning sounds of metal fatigue. Then, a voice behind her.

"Take my hand, Miss. Get into the boat."

Turning to the sound of his voice, she saw a lifeboat with a black number 9 painted on its bow.

She quickly swam to the man tending the boat and climbed aboard.

"What? What is happening?"

"She's going down, Miss," he answered, pointing to a huge ship.

A shocking and unbelievable sight loomed close by. It was the RMS Lusitania. She was listing heavily to the starboard side and going down hard at the bow. Hundreds of passengers were desperately clinging to any debris they could catch to stay afloat. Hundreds of other souls were not as lucky. They floated lifeless in the sea.

Kathryn held her head in disbelief. Nothing made sense at all. How did she get here? Why was she on that ship? Even her clothing appeared foreign to her. She wore a long, dark dress that covered her body to the ankles, and her wet shoes were still laced neatly above them.

Somehow, she had been transported to another time. The year was 1915, and the British-owned Cunard luxury liner had just been torpedoed by a German U-boat.

A single torpedo hit her mid-ship, starboard side. But it was her cargo that caused the greatest damage to her hull. In an effort to support England's war effort against Germany, she had sailed from New York carrying 4 million rounds of American munitions, 5,000 shrapnel shell casings, and percussion artillery fuses in her cargo hold. She was bound for Liverpool, England, but once the torpedo exploded, the Lusitania was doomed. She was going down 20 kilometers off Old Kinsale, southern Ireland.

"How is our patient doing?" asked Dr. Fridrich.

"Much the same, doctor. But her body tenses up frequently and moves about in sudden jerks. She hasn't regained consciousness." the nurse answered with a slow shake of her head.

"Yes, her brain cells are experiencing neurological firings beyond her control. She needs more time."

"We'll take care of her, doctor. She's very special to us here on the 3rd floor."

"I know you will. I'll check back in a few hours. Alert me if anything changes," said Dr. Fridrich as he left the room.

The Lusitania crew valiantly tried to lower the lifeboats, but the ship was going down so fast they didn't have enough time to get them all safely into the water. In the panic, lines broke, and some of them dropped overboard unloaded. Some that were overloaded crashed into the sea nose down, losing all souls. Kathryn witnessed the horror unfolding in front of her knowing that all she could do was pray for them. It was a heartbreaking and sickening scene.

After the ship sank, the lifeboats that had launched successfully were now moving about the sea, combing the water for survivors. There were far too few. Some of them were pulled from the water limp and exhausted, while others, frantic to board the boats, nearly capsized them.

The Lusitania floundered at 2:15 p.m. on May 7, 1915, only 18 minutes after the torpedo exploded. It would take hours to complete their search, even though joined by Irish rescue vessels. Passengers were transferred from the lifeboats in various conditions of shock and injury. The vessels arrived at port later that evening in staggered queue. One by one, they disembarked their passengers onto the pier for thorough processing and proper identification. Many vessels continued throughout the night to bring more survivors to the harbor.

Old Kinsale was closer, but most of the survivors were taken to Queenstown, County Cork. A smaller number were taken to Old Kinsale. Passengers carried their identification on their person at all times while at sea, as well as some of the dead they later discovered. Upon arriving at port, they were properly documented.

When Kathryn was asked for her identification, she searched her pockets. She was relieved to find what she believed were her own documents, although waterlogged, and handed them over to the harbor master. After studying them, he added her name to the list of survivors.

"Welcome to Queenstown, Miss Ryan. We're happy to be of service."

"I beg your pardon?" she asked.

"Welcome to Ireland," he replied, handing the documents back to her.

She quickly took the papers to see for herself, mumbling, "Forgive me. Perhaps I hit my head".

Holding the documents next to the light, she discovered that she was indeed Jean Anne Ryan, an American citizen. A photo of her likeness appeared on the first page.

"Oh, yes. Thank you, sir."

He motioned to someone standing nearby.

"Please escort Miss Ryan to the Queen's Hotel. The accommodations would be more comfortable for a famous American actress," he said with a wink.

She smiled back at him and slowly followed her guide to the hotel. She was exhausted, wet, and cold.

The Queen's was a handsome building with stately décor and furnishings. Jean's notoriety had preceded her arrival. She was graciously received and shown to her suite. Her bedding had been turned down for her, and clean, dry clothing hung in the armoire. A warm nightgown had been placed on the bed as well.

"The maid is coming to draw your bath, Miss, and a hot meal is being prepared for you," said the porter. "You are our guest. Please enjoy a biscuit of fine Irish Whiskey."

The porter gave a quick bow and left her in the suite alone. Jean went to the table and poured a glass of whiskey to steady her nerves. She then walked to a nearby mirror and peered at her reflection. The face staring back at her seemed different, yet somehow familiar.

Not long after, the maid appeared to assist with her bath. She put Jean's shoes next to the heater to dry and bundled her wet clothes to take away for cleaning. The warm water was soothing and welcome. Try as she may, she could not fathom what had happened that day or how she came to be on that doomed ship.

A delicious meal arrived soon after she dressed in her nightgown. Jean ate what she could manage but longed for sleep more than food. The bed was so inviting. She thanked her attendant, and the dishes were quickly taken away. The moment Jean lay herself down, she fell into much-needed sleep.

When morning light filtered into her suite, Jean began to stir. She lazily opened her eyes and slowly stretched her body under the sheets. Looking about her room, she realized she was in a hotel. It took little time for the memory of the terrible day before to rush back into her mind.

She heard the sound of squeaking wheels somewhere outside her window and rose from her bed to investigate. From her window, she saw horse-drawn carts carrying bodies of the dead along the street below. She knew they would be processed by the town's coroner and identified, if possible, then placed in wooden coffins for burial.

She heard a knock at her door and opened it to see her maid smiling brightly.

"Your breakfast, Miss."

Jean gestured for her to enter and watched as she rolled a cart into her suite. The maid placed a traditional Irish breakfast of bangers, scones and hot tea on her table.

"Your clothes are being cleaned and pressed, Miss."

She gave Jean a smile and polite courtesy, then left her room.

After she had eaten, Jean dressed in a freshly ironed blouse and attractive tweed suit. Thankfully, her shoes were dry. She combed and arranged her hair, then left to walk about the town.

Everyone she encountered was respectful and compassionate toward her. She learned that some of the survivors were taken into several homes and given food and clothing until arrangements could be made to get them to their desired destinations.

The townsfolk of Queenstown had experienced many sad occasions in the past as their port was used during the Irish migration to America after the potato famine. America was the shining hope for so many eager to make a new start far from their beloved home.

Jean enjoyed her stroll in the crisp, clean air of the morning and admired rolling hills of the greenest land she'd ever seen. But when she inquired as to the disposition of the deceased, she learned that men were already digging three mass graves, and her mood quickly changed to sorrow.

Three morgues were set up to handle the bodies of the dead men, women, and children for burial. Later that day, identification would be telegraphed to relatives of the victims for further instruction and possible repatriation to their countries of origin. Queenstown had recovered 154 bodies.

Even so, not all of the dead had been retrieved. Bodies would continue to be claimed for days, but it took some even longer to wash ashore at various locations around Ireland and Wales. It was a tragedy of epic proportions, and so soon after the sinking of Lusitania's sister ship, Titanic, three years prior.

News of Germany's terrible attack on a civilian ship hit the headlines in record time and spread worldwide. The names of the survivors and dead were printed in major newspapers all across America. It was reported that Lusitania's manifest contained the names of 1,266 souls that began the voyage to England across the Atlantic. Only 761 survived. 505 had either drowned, went down with the ship, or were simply unclaimed thus far.

When Jean reached the harbor, she noticed that Lusitania's recovered lifeboats were roped together at the slipway. Number 9 was one of them. She recalled her boat carried only five aboard. As she continued her stroll, a strange feeling came to mind. She couldn't really discern what it was. Seemingly, odd flashbacks from another time rushed over her, then faded away just as quickly as they came, leaving her perplexed.

By the time Jean returned to the Queens much later that day, she was immediately greeted at the front desk with news that a telegram had arrived for her. She thanked the clerk and stepped away to a seating area.

She opened the envelope and held the telegram next to a lamp on a nearby table.

It read:

Thank God you are safe. STOP Booking a passage for your return. STOP Sending details soon. STOP Richard. STOP.

She read the words several times and wondered, who is Richard?

CHAPTER 3

Jean chose to take her evening meal in the beautiful hotel dining room that night. The day left her with many deep emotions. She felt grateful to be alive and desired to be in the company of the living. The maitre de seated her at a table with a beautiful view. Twilight had not yet begun. She could hear soft Gaelic music playing from the hotel pub in the next room. It was lovely and lifted her spirits. She wondered how long it would take before returning home. Home, New York?

After reading the menu, she selected the Dover Sole. The waiter stepped away to the kitchen, then returned to her table with a bottle of imported French Chardonay. He opened the bottle, poured a sample into her glass, and waited for Jean's approval.

After taking a sip, she nodded to him, and he filled her glass.

"Thank you," she said.

She noticed a couple at a table nearby looking at her. Moments later, the woman approached Jean's table.

"Please forgive our staring Miss Ryan, but we don't often see a true celebrity in Queenstown. I am Margaret Hopkins. My husband and I wondered if you were continuing on to London to perform for the King."

With some surprise, Jean answered, "I am not quite sure. I don't think it has been decided."

"Of course," remarked Margaret. "The war abroad is giving us all the willies. So pleased you survived the terrible attack. Forgive my intrusion, Miss Ryan."

"Not at all. Thank you for speaking with me."

Unknowingly, the woman had provided much needed information. Jean gave her a beautiful smile, as well as her husband seated the table. As soon as the woman rejoined her husband, the waiter placed Jean's delicately seasoned and prepared fish in front of her. It looked and smelled delicious.

She sipped her wine and savored her meal while a gorgeous sunset appeared outside the window. The music, combined with the soft glow, created a dreamy effect. She would not forget this night.

The next morning, another telegram was delivered to her, and her clothing was returned. Jean sat at her table and pensively drank her tea while she read the telegram.

Play postponed too dangerous. STOP First class passage confirmed RMS Majestic. STOP Departs Queenstown to NY in five days. STOP. Come home. STOP Richard. STOP

She knew the next few days would pass slowly. Again, she questioned, who is Richard? Jean learned that three mass burials were planned for the next day. Lusitania's survivors, as well as Queenstown itself, was in a state of mourning. She would attend the burials to honor her fallen shipmates.

It was Sunday. She heard Church bells somewhere in the distance and decided she would join the townsfolk for service. Perhaps, she would find some peace of mind there. She quickly dressed and inquired at the hotel desk where services would be held.

As she walked along the streets of Queenstown, she noticed that it was bustling with activity, as a great many more people were in the town. Carts carrying additional wooden coffins from Kildare and Dublin had arrived, as well as troops of the Connaught Rangers and Royal Dublin Fusiliers, who were to carry out the burials.

Jean located the ancient stone church and stepped inside. It was standing room only. A tall, Irish gentleman noticed her standing in the back and motioned to her to take his seat near the altar.

"Thank you, so kind," said Jean.

He smiled back at her and stood nearby. Several other survivors were seated near her.

Father Thomas blessed the faithful in attendance and began his sermon. He delivered a stirring tribute for the souls who perished that terrible day. It was so beautiful; Jean was moved to tears. Even so, it was just the solace and released she needed. She joined in singing familiar hymns and left the church at the end of the service feeling uplifted.

The Irish gentleman followed her outside to speak with her.

"Will you attend the burials tomorrow, Miss Ryan?"

"Indeed," she answered, surprised he also knew her identity.

"I work with the Irish Times in Dublin. I was sent here to chronicle the events of the tragedy. Forgive my manners, Miss Ryan. I am Devin Collins."

"So nice to make your acquaintance," responded Jean.

He smiled sweetly and walked along with her.

"Would you join me for lunch, Miss Ryan? I am staying at the Rob Roy."

She considered his offer wondering if it was only for the purpose of an interview. Then she realized he might also provide valuable information to her.

"Why yes, that would be delightful," she decided.

Although not as splendid as the Queen's, the Rob Roy Hotel offered Irish charm and traditional flavor. Upon entering the hotel, Jean was greeted with lively music and delicious smells. The dining room was already at capacity, and they agreed to be put on the waiting list.

"Well then, Miss Ryan, join me in the pub for a pint?" offered Devin.

"Love to," she answered.

They chose a cozy corner booth and began enjoying each other's company.

"Do you plan to travel on to London, Miss Ryan?"

"No, I will return to New York in five days. Richard telegrammed that eastbound travel is not safe."

"Very wise, I agree," said Devin. "A great war is breaking out. Richard Stein is an intelligent man."

"Richard?" she questioned.

"Yes, your agent. I've followed your success on Broadway for many years."

"How kind of you. Will you be staying in Queenstown long, Mr. Collins?"

"I return to Dublin with the others the day after the burial ceremonies tomorrow. Must get the story to press as soon as possible. The world needs to know."

They drank their ale and enjoyed small talk for over an hour until the hostess announced their table was ready in the dining room. By then, Jean was famished, and eagerly followed the hostess.

She immensely enjoyed Devin's company, as well as the ale and delicious shepherd's pie, feeling free to laugh again. They frequently touched each other as they spoke, and the afternoon wore on. He was a breath of fresh air, and she felt alive.

Clearly, an attraction had developed between them. An inevitability would most certainly take its course. Jean allowed Devin to walk her to her hotel. Although she knew she had had too much to drink, she tried to convince him she could handle it. Even so, Devin escorted her to her suite and helped her inside. Reaching up to him to bid goodnight, she touched his face and longingly looked into his eyes. Devin responded in like fashion. Taking her by the shoulders, he slowly moved Jean backward toward the bed.

Without hesitation, she breathed, "Yes."

The nurse alerted Dr. Fridrich when Kathryn's rate of respiration suddenly increased, and her blood pressure raised dramatically. The doctor checked her vital signs, and they observed Kathryn's behavior for several minutes until the monitors returned to normal.

"Doctor, is she smiling?" she asked.

"I believe so," he answered. "A good sign she's still with us. Let's stay the course."

Jean and Devin made love long into the night until shear exhaustion and sleep left them lying together in each other's arms. By morning, Jean found herself alone and naked in her bed. The carnal pleasures of the night before still lingered, and she gently caressed the contours of her body until a knock at the door brought her to her feet. She quickly slipped on her nightgown and went to the door.

Her maid cheerfully greeted her, "Morning, Miss, breakfast."

"Good morning, Alice. Please come in."

The maid placed hot tea and covered plates on Jean's table by the window.

"The ceremonies will begin early this morning, Miss," Alice informed. "Will there be anything else?"

Jean lifted the lid from her plate and was delighted to see scrambled eggs and warm biscuits with honey. "Yes, Alice, I would like a bath."

"Right, Miss. Please enjoy your breakfast. I will return with fresh towels straight away."

Jean relished her warm bath, then took the cleaned clothes she last wore on the Lusitania from the armoire. She dressed and neatly arranged her hair. Taking the long dark coat provided for her from the hanger, she left the room and went downstairs.

This time, she didn't need to ask directions, she simply followed the ceremonial procession of coffins in makeshift hearses down the street. The Connaught Rangers and Dublin Fusiliers smartly marched alongside. The gravesite contained three enormous graves. One at a time, the wooden coffins were lowered into the graves and tightly packed.

When he saw her, Father Thomas ushered Jean to a place of respect near the opening. Devin came to her side and stood with her.

Father Thomas gave the last rights throughout the morning and into the afternoon while the throng of mourners joined in prayer and song. It was a deeply somber scene, palpable and heart-wrenching.

When the burials ended, the souls of the dead rested together in perpetual slumber.

Jean and Devin quietly walked through the town and sat together on a bench by the harbor, far away from the sadness. The Dublin Fusiliers, as well as hundreds of others busily boarded Devin's ship.

"I can't stay, Jean. I wish I could, but a storm is reported to be headed this way. The ship's captain wants everyone to be boarded and underway within the hour. We need to return to Dublin before the storm arrives."

"Of course, I understand."

"You will see your Richard in a few days. He's a lucky man."

Jean slowly shook her head.

"I don't believe he is my Richard."

Except for noisy seagulls swooping overhead, they sat together, observing the ship's activities in silence. Soon, the ship's horn announced last boarding call.

"That's my cue, as they say," remarked Devin.

"You must go," Jean answered.

Slowly, they walked to the gangway and stopped. They stared into each other's eyes for a moment, wondering what might have been.

Devin leaned down and held her in a long embrace.

"I will never forget you, Jean Ryan."

"I enjoyed your company, Mr. Collins," she whispered back. "Safe journey."

Devin boarded the ship, and Jean returned to her seat on the bench.

Not long after, ship's engines came to life, and the mooring lines were dropped. Jean watched as the ship maneuvered in the harbor and headed out to sea, watching until the ship finally dipped below the horizon. She looked skyward to the west. Clouds had already begun to darken. She decided it was time to return to her hotel.

CHAPTER 4

The storm rushed in overnight and heavy rain began the next day. Jean sat by her window, looking out at the gloom. Queenstown appeared empty and abandoned. The rain would continue into the night. Two days remained before the RMS Majestic arrived. It would depart on Friday, the day after, for the mainland. She would try to keep herself occupied to pass the time.

Perhaps she would visit with Father Thomas to learn the history of the town, spend quiet moments walking along the seashore. Or, perhaps, take a short journey into the countryside. She would make good use of the time left in Ireland, and her freedom, to do as she pleased.

For some reason, she had an uneasy feeling about her return to New York and Richard Stein.

At noon she took her lunch in the hotel dining room. Although the maitre de happily sat her at the table she had before by the window; the view was no longer as splendid. It was a dark, cold, wet day, and rain water filled the streets. Occasionally, a brave soul darted across the street to a building nearby.

She chose a simple plate of fish and chips and a cold ale from the pub.

In her effort to cheer the guests, a harpist, who sat in the corner of the dining room, played beautiful Irish ballads. The waiter soon brought a pint of cold ale to her table.

"Enjoy, Miss."

"Thank you," she smiled.

With the first sip, she immediately remembered her happy day and night with Devin. Solitude has its benefits, but after all that she'd been through the past several days, he was the lifeline she desperately needed, a return to the living and her inner desires. Jean knew they would never meet again. Even so, she would be forever grateful he came into her life.

Again, the front desk clerk delivered a telegram. She thought to herself, "Now what?" She opened the envelope and held it next to the lamp on her table.

It read:

Great News! STOP. You have the Lead in Charles Klein's new play, Cousin Lucy! STOP Opens August 27 George M. Cohan's Theatre. STOP Music by Jerome Kern. STOP Congratulations! Broadway thrilled to see you. STOP Richard. STOP

Jean was stunned and quickly took a long drink of ale. She shook her head in disbelief. She had no idea how to react to this news. She stared out the window, looking for an answer. She simply could not remember her life in New York. Was she capable of such a performance?

She gestured to her waiter to bring another ale and quickly finished the one in front of her. Thankfully, the beautiful music helped to calm her anxiety.

The waiter delivered a golden brown meal to her table and another ale. It was delicious, but she ate slowly, preoccupied with the telegram. She needed someone she could trust to confide in. Tomorrow, after the storm front moved out, she would talk with Father Thomas.

The following day, Jean walked to the church with a sense of purpose and resolve.

Father Thomas was pleased to see her and immediately blessed her with the sign of the cross. He led her to a pew near the altar and asked her to sit with him. It was quiet and reverent there, and she felt comforted. It was exactly what she needed.

"I see you are troubled, my child. How may I help you?"

"Yes, Father, I don't seem to know what has happened to me," she answered.

"You have experienced a terrible thing. God has saved you for a reason, a reason known only to Him. It is not our place to understand His plan but accept the blessings He gives us. God wants you to live your life, my child."

"That's just it. My life does not feel real, Father."

"It will in time. You must have faith."

They sat silently for several moments. Jean looked at the altar and the crucifix on the wall.

With a slow nod, Jean responded, "I will do my best, Father. Thank you for listening."

"I am here for you whenever you need me," said Father Thomas.

He made the sign of the cross upon her forehead.

"Bless this woman of God."

"Thank you, Father," said Jean.

Father Thomas escorted her out of the church and waved goodbye with a gentle smile.

Jean walked along the seashore breathing in the fresh sea air, and enjoying the peaceful sound of the ocean. Billowy clouds gently floated across the panoramic sea and Irish coastline. It was a gorgeous day.

As she walked the beach, she picked up shells and rocks she found interesting. One stone, in particular, caught her attention. It was a beautiful white stone that sparkled with mica schist on all sides and two crannies of geode tucked inside. It fit perfectly into the palm of her hand. She washed the stone in a wave and sat down on a nearby rock protruding from the sand.

Her ship would arrive tomorrow. She took a deep breath of sea air and dreaded the thought of leaving this beautiful place of refuge. It was a blessing in many ways. Jean remained by the sea all day with the stone resting in her lap until the sunset lost its beautiful hues.

When she returned to her hotel, she asked that her evening meal be brought to her suite. As always, her bed had been turned down, and a fresh nightgown was ready for her. Soon after, a delicious dinner was delivered with a bottle of wine. She slowly enjoyed her meal while the wine warmed her body. After two glasses, she decided to retire early. She simply could not shake the anxiety of returning to New York. Thankfully, the fresh air of the day took little time to work its magic, and she drifted off to sleep as soon as her head rested on the pillow.

By morning, the RMS Majestic was anchored in the harbor. Jean could see the top of her smokestack from her hotel window. Again, a feeling of dread washed over her.

Alice greeted Jean with breakfast and tea and asked if she could bring her anything else.

"Yes, I will need a small bag or satchel to take with me on the ship. I must prepare for the voyage."

"Straight away, Miss," answered Alice with her usual cheerful smile. "I'll take care of everything."

Later that morning, Jean visited the gravesites once more. The heavy rain had packed down the soil of the fresh graves. Queenstown had erected a large marble headstone next to the graves with the names of the dead inscribed on a metal plaque. Jean touched the plaque and silently read the names of her shipmates. The cemetery was vacant of other visitors, so she sat for a moment on the stone bench nearby. Only an occasional breeze joined her solitude. Finally, with a heavy heart, she said her final farewell and returned to her hotel, where she remained the rest of the day.

Jean boarded the RMS Majestic and was escorted to her stateroom. She quickly settled in and joined other travelers on the promenade deck just as the ship got underway. Some of the townsfolk stood on the pier waving goodbye. She was humbled to see Alice among them with her usual cheerful smile. Jean smiled down at her and blew a kiss. She would miss this beautiful emerald isle and its wonderful people.

Gratefully, the voyage was uneventful. The Majestic docked at the Port of New York in only a few days. When she disembarked, Jean noticed a nicely dressed man with a thin black mustache busily ordering people about.

He quickly approached her and said, "Welcome home, Jean."

She returned his welcome with a half-smile.

"Mr. Stein, will there be any other luggage?" said the taxi driver taking Jean's bag.

"No, this is all," Jean answered.

So this was Richard. She instantly felt uneasy and wary.

All the way to her flat, Richard talked about the play. She thought it odd he didn't even inquire as to her health or Lusitania's sinking. When they arrived, he joined her in her stylish apartment, then immediately helped himself to a scotch at her wet bar.

"Shall I pour one for you?" he asked.

"Please do." She had a feeling she would need it.

He handed her the glass and said, "Let's talk about production."

Jean took a long sip and sat down in her chair.

"I'm not ready, Richard."

"What do you mean? Not ready to talk?"

"No, I'm not ready to do this. I'm not ready for Broadway."

Richard instantly clenched his jaw. "What was that? Of course, you are, and you must."

"I just can't do it, I'm not ready. I need more time," she implored.

"You can and you will!" he roared. "I worked hard to broker this part. Costume fittings begin tomorrow; playbills are already designed. Broadway welcomes you home with open arms."

"Richard, you don't understand," she repeated, walking toward him. "I need more time."

"You don't have the time," he said, pushing her back into the chair.

"Get out, Richard," Jean demanded, again rising from her chair.

He became enraged and pushed her into the chair harder. She immediately kicked him in the groin, and he backed off.

"It's my life!"

As soon as his pain subsided, he slapped her hard across the face.

"Get out! We're through, Richard. Get out!"

"Are you trying to ruin my reputation? I own you! Your life belongs to me!"

He dragged her out of the chair and threw her on the floor. Jean tried to push him away. His face was red with anger, and he grabbed her throat. The harder she tried to fight back, the more he tightened his grip.

She struggled to breath. She was helpless against his enraged strength.

"Richard, stop. Can't breathe."

Within seconds, she spiraled out of consciousness.

Kathryn's rate of respiration became alarmingly erratic, and the nurse quickly applied an oxygen mask. But Kathryn was unreceptive.

"Call Dr. Fridrich. I need him now!"

The medical staff quickly went into emergency mode. They injected Kathryn with stimulants, but she didn't respond. Her life was failing. Numbers on the monitors steadily dropped until they flat-lined. The nurse began CPR until a defibrillator was quickly brought to Kathryn's bedside. After two lifesaving jolts were delivered to her heart, the monitors indicated restored levels of life.

Dr. Fridrich soon joined them.

Kathryn was breathing again but still unconscious.

"Excellent work, team."

He stayed with Kathryn for several minutes until he became convinced her heart was stable. With appreciation, he touched the nurses' shoulders.

"Continue to maintain oxygen and monitor her vitals. She's come this far; we're not going to lose her now. Keep me informed."

She convulsively tried to cough out the thick smoke from her lungs.

"Hang on, Alison Taylor, I'll get you out of here."

She could feel the strong hands of someone dragging her out of a burning building.

CHAPTER 5

Even though her eyes burned from the smoke, she could make out the body of her rescuer lying against her, shot dead. Alison was terrified and quickly got to her feet to run, but she couldn't see clearly and stumble to the ground.

Animals were screaming and on fire. A massacre was underway. People were dying or dead, shot with rifles and arrows by a barrage of weapons' fire that came from every direction by men on horseback and on the walls.

Fort Henry was on fire and mercilessly under siege. A band of renegades, consisting of outlaws and Native Americans, had successfully breached the entrance, making escape impossible. The Oklahoma and Texas plains were Comanche territory, where Mexicans and Civil War deserters were eager to join in the pillage and destruction for profit. They knew that native tribes would take the blame, leaving them free to run.

Alison lay there hoping to make herself inconspicuous, curled in the fetal position to protect her core, silently praying for her life. Within several minutes' gunshots finally subsided. Unattended, the fires continued to burn inside the fort. She could hear men talking and shouting in a frenzy of slaughter and victory. One of them kicked her in the back, and she cried out in pain.

"This one is still alive," yelled a man with a thick Mexican accent.

He was joined by a white man who observed her lying on the ground.

"We'll take her with us. We can sell her."

After the fort smoldered to the ground, Alison was bound and roughly thrown over the back of a horse.

The Mexican rubbed her buttocks and said, "I will have you tonight."

"Chico," shouted the white man. "Get on your horse."

"Si, Amigo," he complied, grinning back at Alison with a chuckle and a whoop.

The long ride to their camp was grueling for Alison. She was hot, nauseous, and in pain. Her rib cage felt as if it would crack at any moment. The hot and sweaty animal beneath her made her discomfort all the more unpleasant.

When they finally reached the camp, the sun was setting in the west. She was taken off the horse, carried to a nearby tree to rest, and given water. As nightfall began, the men drank heavily and talked loudly among themselves until, one by one, they fell asleep. Alison nervously watched the men, afraid to close her eyes, until fatigue brought her to rest.

Much later in the night, she sensed someone was near her. She felt the rope around her ankles loosen and her shoes removed from her feet. Her hands were left bound. Slowly, her skirts were pulled up over her waist, and a hand reached her genitals.

It was Chico. He had kept his promise.

He removed his belt and forced her legs apart with his body. He wreaked with the foul smell of sweat and mezcal, and took little time to penetrate her. Alison tried to scream and get away from him, but his hand tightly covered her mouth, and his strength prevented her movement. He grunted repeatedly while he rammed himself inside of her.

She was helplessly pinned to the ground. Silent tears ran down her face.

After he was spent, he rolled off of her and onto his back.

"Muy bueno, bello," he sighed before passing out.

No one else in the camp was awake.

Under the darkness of night and still bound, Alison took flight. She had no idea where she was going. She just needed to get as far away from the men as fast as she could. Her bare feet were cut and bleeding as she ran through the rocks and brush along the way until a crust of dirt and sand covered them.

At daybreak, she stopped to rest close to a bolder along a hillside. As she leaned against the stone, she enjoyed the beautiful colors of sunlight rising from the east. She was alone on the prairie and felt safe enough to close her eyes.

A few short hours later, she was jolted awake by the sound and vibration of a heavy, running animal. It was a steer, and it was running away from something.

Alison sat erect and looked all around her. What was it? Suddenly, a horse and rider jumped passed her at full speed in pursuit of the steer. The rider was a cowboy determined to return the animal to the herd.

She stood to get his attention. As he drove the steer back up the hillside, he spotted Alison and abruptly turned his horse toward her.

"Thanks be to God," she murmured.

The cowboy stopped his horse and took off his hat.

"Howdy, Ma'am. Are you lost? May I be of assistance?"

"Yes, yes, please. I'm hurt, and I need help," she answered.

He dismounted and carefully cut the leather strap around her wrists.

"I'm Travis, Ma'am. I work for the Fallon Ranch. We're driving a herd up from Mexico. Let me put you on my horse and take you to Mr. Fallon. He'll know what to do."

Alison gratefully nodded to him and broke into tears. He gently lifted her onto his horse and walked both of them back to the herd that rested in the valley beyond the ridge. Along the way, she told him about the attack at Fort Henry, that she was the only one that got out alive. Travis knew she was severely weak and needed water. He steadied her in the saddle all the way.

When they reached the chuck wagon, he helped her dismount and sat her down against a wheel. The cook came alongside of her and handed her a canteen full of water. Others joined the wagon to learn what had happened, and soon the boss arrived. Travis walked up to him and told him what he knew about her.

John Fallon got off his horse, took off his hat, and approached Alison.

"I'm Fallon, Ma'am. We'll take good care of you. My ranch is only a day away. You will get the attention you need there. Cookie, give Miss Taylor something to eat, and Travis, stay with her. Give her whatever she wants."

"Yes, sir, Mr. Fallon," Travis responded. He removed his hat again and added, "It would be an honor, Ma'am."

Fallon's housekeeper, Maria, waited on the porch as they drove up to the ranch house. She helped Alison down from the wagon and cradled an arm around her.

"Senora, come with me. I take care of you," Maria said soothingly.

They entered the large doorway and stepped inside Fallon's beautiful home.

"Please," begged Alison, "I need a bath."

She pointed to her groin with tears in her eyes.

"I was attacked."

"Si, Senora, no worry. I'll bring you medicine. No worry, Senora."

Maria knew what to do to prevent an unwanted pregnancy. After taking Alison to her room, she left to prepare the substance to be inserted. When she returned, she helped Alison cleanse herself deep inside with the solution. She assured her it was a natural remedy that was known to be safe and effective. Yet, it was painful to insert due to the injury suffered from forced entry, only time would tell if it would succeed.

Maria bathed and tended to Alison throughout the day and rubbed medicine on her wounded feet. Fresh clothing and moccasins were left for her to wear.

"You rest now, Senora. I'll come for you later," Maria said softly, then left Alison in the room alone.

Later that evening, she was invited to dinner with John Fallon and his wife. It was a sumptuous meal prepared and served by Maria. John inquired as to her harrowing experience at the fort. Alison told them everything she could remember.

"Savages," responded Emily Fallon with disgust. "We heard the Comanche are on the warpath."

"Perhaps so," replied Alison. "But the men who burned Fort Henry were not Indians. They were mostly outlaws and renegades."

"Si, Senor Fallon, and she was attacked by one of them," offered Maria, with hopes Fallon would defend her honor.

Alison lowered her eyes and nodded with shame.

"Not your fault, my dear," offered Emily.

"Who was the dastardly cad that did that? Do you know his name?" demanded John.

"He was a Mexican. Someone called him Chico."

Maria opened her eyes with surprise and said, "I know this Chico. Si, he is a bad man. He runs with bad men."

"Do you know where he goes to hide, Maria?"

"Si, Senor Fallon. The Waco territory."

"I'll send word to the Texas Rangers in Austin. We'll hunt them down and bring them all to justice."

Emily smiled at John with love and pride. She knew her husband would complete the task.

"Thank you, Mr. Fallon, thank you." said Alison.

In two days' time, news of the atrocity at Fort Henry spread throughout the territory by telegraph, reaching far and wide across the country.

Soon, five Texas Rangers arrived at the Fallon Ranch to talk to John and Alison, the lone survivor.

When they learned what they needed, Fallon and several of his men were deputized. Together, they set out for the Waco territory before sunset. Fallon left Travis and six men behind to protect the ranch.

Alison spent the next few days discovering the splendor of the sprawling ranch and enjoying long walks with Travis. Yet, she just couldn't understand why she had the feeling that she wasn't supposed to be there. The memory of her past was cloudy at best. Only the trauma of recent events seemed to exist. Perhaps it would return to her in time.

Emily and Alison were rocking comfortably on the long porch when a rider approached. Emily stood to greet him.

"We got them, Mrs. Fallon. The men that are still alive were taken to Austin. They are behind bars. Mr. Fallon wants Miss Taylor to come to Austin as the key witness in their trial."

"Thank you for the good news. Please water your horse and refresh yourself. Travis and two men will accompany Miss Taylor and me to Austin tomorrow. Please stay behind and care for the ranch.

"Yes, Ma'am."

"Maria, please help Alison prepare for the journey."

"Si, Senora, I do for her," Maria responded with a broad smile.

Austin was very busy and growing by leaps and bounds. People came to town to see the trial of the ruthless gang of misfits and murderers known as the Gringos. The outcome of the trial would most certainly be a mass hanging. The trial was set to begin as soon as the star witness arrived. By the next morning, ten prisoners entered the courthouse heavily guarded and were seated in chairs along the wall.

When Alison walked into the courtroom, she was ushered to the witness stand. She could hear Chico snickering at her, unsettling her nerve. The judge immediately gaveled him to be silenced. He instructed Alison to look at the men and identify whether they were the ones that destroyed Fort Henry and murdered the men, women, and children inside.

She slowly looked at each man. Chico continued to sneer back at her. Then she nodded her head.

"Yes, your honor, they are the ones that did it," she confirmed.

Alison was allowed to leave the courtroom first for her safety. As she walked through the door, she heard the judge sentence them all to hang by the neck until dead.

"Hanging to commence forthwith," ordered the judge as he gaveled the trial ended.

The gallows had been prepared the day before, and a large crowd gathered to bear witness to swift justice. Alison and Emily would watch the hanging from the safety of their hotel window.

It was a grisly sight, but Alison felt vindicated when it was over, and their bodies were taken away. They sat together in silence for several moments until John Fallon entered the room.

He walked up to Alison and removed his hat.

"It is over, Miss Taylor. It is done."

"Thank you, Mr. Fallon," she replied.

John invited both of them to join him for lunch at a table he had reserved in the dining room.

After they were seated, a man approached their table.

"Miss Alison Taylor?" he inquired.

"Yes, she is," responded Emily. "And you are?"

He introduced himself as Detective Lewis Franks with the Bay Area Detective Agency in San Francisco, California. He explained that he had been hired by her Aunt, Elizabeth Langley. He had been paid to find her and deliver her to San Francisco in person, that Alison's unfortunate experience occurred while she was in route to live with her.

"Why? that's wonderful," said Emily, smiling broadly at Alison.

It was evident that news of the massacre had reached the west coast. Her Aunt was eager to see that her niece complete her journey safe and sound. He was to escort Alison by rail the rest of the way. A westbound train would arrive the next day, departing Austin by noon. Alison agreed to go with him. But she didn't know how to react, and she lowered her eyes with a frown.

"What is troubling you, my dear?" asked Emily.

"Mrs. Fallon. I don't seem to remember my aunt. I can't really remember anything before Fort Henry. Is there something wrong with me?"

Emily consoled Alison and softly touched her shoulder.

"Of course not, my dear. It was a terrible, traumatic experience. But you are strong and alive. Just be brave and go with your heart."

"I'm not sure how," said Alison.

"You will learn what to do. I'm sure your aunt loves you very much. Remember, you will always be welcome with us for as long as you wish if you care to return. Go with God."

CHAPTER 6

Aunt Beth was known as Lady Elizabeth Langley within San Francisco society. She was a widow and the sole heir to a gold mine. She was refined and lived in a stately home on Nob Hill. Elizabeth was full of life and vigor. She intended to take Alison under her wing to show her the city and all its magic.

Once the train came to a stop at the station, she waited excitedly for her niece to step on the platform. Her driver held a sign with Alison's name. Elizabeth had only seen Alison once, when she was a baby. Now that she was the only living family she had since the death of her sister, she insisted that Alison come live with her.

When Alison saw her name, she went to the woman and man standing in wait.

"I am Alison Taylor," she said.

Delighted to see her niece again, she immediately gave her a warm embrace with an enormous smile.

"My dear Alison, you look exactly like your mother, God rest her soul. Come with us now. Let's get you home."

Elizabeth rushed her away from the station, and they climbed aboard her carriage.

"I have so much to show you. We'll have great fun together. You can call me Aunt Beth."

It was a perfect, cloudless day, and the pristine San Francisco Bay sparkled in the sunlight. Alison gratefully breathed in the fresh, cool sea air. She marveled at all the tall ships moored along the numerous piers in the bay. She would be eager to visit them one day.

Aunt Beth was her deceased mother's only sister. Alison had no siblings, and Elizabeth had no children. It would be a perfect arrangement for both of them. As they rode along in the carriage, Elizabeth noticed the clothing her niece was wearing.

"I think the first order of things is to get you some new clothes, my dear. I'll send for my seamstress in the morning," she said with a wink.

A cable car took them up Nob Hill to a waiting carriage that delivered them to Elizabeth's home.

Alison was amazed by its beauty and size. It was truly fit for an heiress to a gold mine.

After Alison settled in and bathed, she joined her aunt on the veranda overlooking the beautiful bay. The maid brought refreshments to their table, and they got to know each other as they talked for hours.

Elizabeth did not question Alison about her harrowing experience at Fort Henry or the trial. She knew it was a painful ordeal and would not bring up the subject until Alison wanted to talk about it.

Dinner was served at six with wine and delicious desserts, but Alison soon became exhausted after her meal and bid her aunt a sweet goodnight in the early evening.

She awoke the next morning eager for new sights and adventure. Aunt Beth joined her for breakfast, and they discussed where they should visit first. There was so much to see and do in San Francisco, a multi-culture city rich with charm and promise.

Alison was intrigued with the tall ships moored and anchored in the bay along the waterfront. She learned that the shipping docks also offered ferry boats to transport travelers to and from the town of Vallejo and up-valley.

Chinatown offered exotic smells, foods, and flavors. Where jades, gems, and stunning artistic carvings were for sale, almost like visiting the faraway land itself. Its population and culture was rapidly growing and establishing permanence in San Francisco for generations to come.

The long seaside coastline on its westernmost side was the perfect place for long strolls and enjoyment in the sea. Yet, San Francisco's beginnings were lawless, severe, and dangerous, a wide-open city. The gold rush of 1849 had corruptly filled the city with graft, gambling, drinking, prostitution, and crime. It was known as The Barberry Coast. Now it was becoming more refined and civilized.

Alison truly enjoyed her breakfast with Aunt Beth. She already felt safe and comfortable there. She was ready to explore.

Before noon, Elisabeth's seamstress arrived. Alison's measurements were taken, and beautiful bolts of material were displayed for her to choose from. Elizabeth was planning a fabulous dinner party at the Palace Hotel on Montgomery Street that would take place a week later. She would invite only the most influential of San Francisco society as she intended to show off her niece in grand style.

The next day Elizabeth's carriage took them to the wharf. Alison was amazed by the heavy, salty odor of the fishing ships unloading their catch of Dungeness crab and all types of shrimp and fish fresh from the ocean. It was a smell forever to be imprinted on her mind.

Elizabeth purchased several of the creatures and had them taken directly to her chef. They would enjoy a feast that night. Alison and her aunt walked along the waterfront together, admiring the vessels in the water. There were so many of them lined up.

"Aunt Beth, where do all these ships come from?"

"All over the world, my dear. The ocean is vast, and many of these tall ships bring spices and goods from all over the exotic islands of the South Pacific. Some carry passengers. I know a certain captain quite well who sails several of these ships year-round. He is the wealthy owner of the South Sea Shipping Company. You will meet him at the dinner party," she looked at Alison with a smile and added, "Quite handsome as well."

Alison smiled back at her aunt, somewhat flushed, and raised her eyebrows with interest.

That evening, Alison enjoyed the most wonderful crab and seafood she'd ever tasted with a wonderful bottle of wine by candlelight. They watched a glorious sunset together until it disappeared beyond the horizon. She felt loved and safe, grateful for her Aunt Beth and good fortune. Her companionship was a gift from God.

Alison visited the seashore alone several times during the next few days. She wanted to distance herself from the memory of the tragic events she encountered at Fort Henry. The fresh sea air was the perfect antidote, yet the lost memory of her past was extremely troubling as she couldn't even remember her mother.

Soon the day of the dinner party arrived. Alison loved her beautiful gown, and Elizabeth delighted herself in fussing over her. She presented her niece with a gorgeous pearl necklace and made sure her hair was arranged in the highest fashion. They stepped into the carriage and rode to the Palace Hotel.

They passed many buildings along the way. Elizabeth pointed out several places they would visit at a later time. When they arrived at the Palace, they were escorted to the main dining room. Soft music entertained the guests seated at the tables.

Alison's entrance was met with smiles and hushed sounds of approval. She looked stunning and beautiful. One by one, Elizabeth introduced her guests to her niece, and adoration was immediate with all whom she met. One man, in particular, caught Alison's attention. He was standing to the side, watching every smile she made with each introduction. Her eyes turned to him intermittently, wondering who he was. Finally, he approached her, wine glass in hand.

"Alison, this is Captain Andrew Bryant. He owns a shipping line with a fleet of vessels."

She demurely smiled at him, just as a waiter offered her a glass of wine on a shining silver tray. As they looked at each other, a mutual attraction began to build.

Elizabeth smiled broadly and said, "I'll leave you two to get acquainted."

Another guest took Elizabeth's arm, and she walked away with her.

"You look enchanting this evening, Miss Taylor," said Capt. Bryant, lifting his glass of wine to her.

Alison smiled at him.

"You look dashing as well, Captain Bryant," she responded, lifting her glass to him.

They both took a sip of their wine without taking their eyes away from each other. They talked for several minutes before being seated for dinner. Elizabeth had planned the seating arrangements. She intentionally seated them together. It was a marvelous affair. Alison felt special and alive, like a princess at a ball.

As they savored their delicious repast and wine together, Alison became more attracted to the Captain.

"Tell me, Captain Bryant, do you sail to the south seas often?"

"Why? yes," he answered, leaning closer to her. "Please call me Andrew, your aunt does."

Alison smiled and agreed to do so.

"Please call me Alison," she said with a grin.

"Indeed."

The music and magic of the evening played on until the event came to an end.

"May I escort your niece home, Elizabeth?"

"Of course, Andrew," she said with a wink. "After all, the night is still young."

Alison and Andrew left the Palace Hotel and waited for a carriage outside its fabulous entrance. When it arrived, Alison hesitated to board and turned to him.

"Must you take me home, Andrew? I would love to see your ship in the moonlight."

"Excellent suggestion, Alison. Driver, take us to the wharf."

Streetlights lined the buildings and taverns along the waterfront. Andrew's ship was well-lighted and rocked gently against the pier.

"Would you care for a little late-night entertainment and an ale, Miss Taylor? he asked. "Then I'll take you aboard my ship."

"Love to, Captain," she responded.

They walked across the street to his favorite tavern. The music played loudly, and the people inside danced and laughed in merriment. It was a bawdy, unrefined establishment, but Alison felt free to let her hair down and join in all the fun.

She danced and drank with Andrew for hours until it was time to leave. She had consumed more than one ale, so the fresh evening air would do her good.

Andrew took her to his ship and carefully guided her up the gangway. She had become quite tipsy. It was quiet aboard ship. Most of the seamen were ashore. Three hands guarded the pier and lighted gangway. Alison was impressed by the beauty and cleanliness of his ship.

"And where are your quarters, sir?" she asked.

Andrew smiled and answered, "Allow me to show you."

Once inside, they could no longer avoid each other. They quickly disrobed and joined their bodies on his bed. Their passion had no bounds, and they made deep, sensual love while the ship gently rocked at its mooring.

When the early morning bell sounded, Andrew knew it was 4 a.m.

He gently awakened Alison, stroking her nakedness, and said, "Good morning, sweet love. I must get you home to Elizabeth before the sun rises. A lady should not be seen in daylight wearing her evening gown."

CHAPTER 7

Alison slept late that morning. By the time she joined Aunt Beth for her breakfast, she had acquired a pounding headache.

Elizabeth smiled sympathetically at her niece.

"I see you enjoyed yourself last night. You were beautiful."

"Thank you, Aunt Beth. It was the most wonderful night of my life and then some," she said, holding her head in her hand.

"Well then, perhaps we should have a nice hot toddy this morning. That should revive your spirits."

"Yes, please," Alison chuckled apologetically.

San Francisco became an endless playground for Alison and Elizabeth. Shopping jaunts, exploration, and ladies' luncheons were the highlights of the next several days.

Andrew visited often. During the moonlit hours, they fell madly in love. Every moment together was treasured. Andrew took her to the tavern twice more, and twice more, they made love with wild abandon aboard his ship. Then, all too soon, Andrew had to set sail for the islands. It would be several weeks before his return.

Elizabeth could easily see that Alison was brokenhearted. A new opera was opening soon, so she purchased two tickets for opening night. It was a comedy, and it would be good to see Alison laugh again.

That evening, the opera was a great success. They both enjoyed themselves immensely. When it ended, they joined several others outside the opera house and shared their approval of the performance while waiting for their carriages to come for them. It was a warm, beautiful night, yet there was a strange silence.

Suddenly, the ground began to shake violently. It was an earthquake. Tremors rolled beneath the cobblestone streets as shock waves came in rapid succession. A team of horses pulling a carriage became terrified and broke into a rundown Montgomery Street. Elizabeth held onto Alison for balance, but by the time the carriage reached them, it had flipped on its side, barreling toward them. Alison forcefully pushed her aunt out of the way just as the carriage slammed into her abdomen, crushing her against a light post. She cried out with unbearable pain. Then, the world began spinning and spiraling out of control again.

"Mary, you need to stop pushing. The baby isn't ready yet," coached the midwife attending her.

Mary was lying in a pool of sweat. She had been in labor for hours, and the pain was terrible. She was in a log cabin. A man knelt beside her holding her hand. He was Mary's husband.

"Jack, her pain is bad. The baby isn't responding normally," said the midwife.

"Doctor, Kathryn is in crisis. She's experiencing a great deal of pain, but I can't tell what's causing it. Her rate of respiration has skyrocketed."

"Yes, she is having some kind of crisis. But I don't believe it is physical. I think it's all in her mind," said Dr. Fridrich. "This has gone on too long. We need to get her back now."

The doctor injected Kathryn with a powerful stimulant. He observed her reaction as she slowly returned to consciousness.

"Where have you been, Kathryn?" he asked. "We've been waiting for you."

Kathryn opened her eyes and began to sob.

"Not possible, why, why? What have you done to me?"

The doctor and nurse looked at each other in disbelief. They have no words.

"My baby, my baby."

Her sorrow was real. Tears ran down her face.

The nurse touched her shoulder.

"Your baby is fine, Kathryn," she said softly. "Your little girl is safe with your sister, Jacqueline. Melissa is safe, Kathryn. They have been waiting for you to get well. You've been on an odyssey."

"You beat Covid, Kathryn. It's gone now," added the doctor. "You'll see your sister and daughter in a few hours. Let's see if we can get you to drink some juice now."

This time, the doctor's eyes did not send Kathryn into panic, and the nurse gently wiped away her tears. The monitors confirmed that her vital signs had returned to normal levels. The danger was finally over. Kathryn's memories flooded back to her as she knew this existence was where she belonged.

In a few hours, they moved Kathryn out of ICU and into a private room for the remainder of her recovery.

"After you are able to ingest food and ambulate on your own, the doctor will release you to your sister's care," the nurse informed her.

Kathryn nodded with appreciation.

When she settled in, Jackie and Melissa were allowed to see her.

"Mommy!" yelled Missy.

"Hi, pumpkin, I missed you," said Kathryn.

"I missed you too, Mommy," she gave Kathryn a hug and continued, "I have a new purse. Aunt Jackie got me a new purse."

"Very pretty purse, sweetheart."

"And a little kitty," Missy added, pulling a small plush toy from her purse.

"Very sweet," she said, smiling at Jackie.

"Jackie, thank you so much for taking care of Missy for me. Thank you for everything you've done for us, love you very much."

"Love you too, Sis. That's what family does. Besides, Matt loved having a little one in our big empty house. When you're released, you'll stay with us for a few more days, okay?"

"Sure, that sounds really nice."

They were allowed to visit for only a half hour. She needed to get her strength back.

Kathryn had divorced her ex the year before. He was a pilot for a major airline out of Chicago who kept mistresses at every layover destination. As a single mom, raising a child alone had its moments, but the divorce settlement provided handsomely for both of them, as well as the child support she received. Jackie and Matt were an added bonus, always available to help. They all lived close to each other in Park Ridge, a suburb of Chicago.

Kathryn's recovery went extremely well, and she was released in less than a week. Dr. Fridrich examined her again that last day. He cheerfully congratulated her good health and asked if he could do anything else for her.

"Yes, please, doctor. I need to talk to someone. Someone who can explain what happened to my brain."

"You certainly deserve some answers. I'm going to refer you to the best neurologist in the business at the Neurological Institute in Chicago. His name is Dr. Robert Simons. I'll see that you have the number to his office with your discharge papers and contact them for an appointment when you are ready."

"Thank you, doctor, thank you very much. I am eternally grateful for all of you."

The nursing staff seated Kathryn in a wheelchair and escorted her to the hospital exit. They cheered her all the way. Jackie met her outside the hospital, helped her into her car, and drove to her home. Matt and Missy met them the moment they arrived.

Kathryn was thrilled to be out of the hospital. She was delighted to make herself comfortable in a real house again.

She got stronger every day, yet the cloudy flashbacks of something she couldn't define, couldn't explain, continued to come and go. She discussed what she could remember with Jackie and told her about the referral to see the neurologist. They both agreed that she should make the appointment much sooner than later.

"Kate, I'll drive you to the Institute, and Matt can watch Missy."

Kathryn soon met with Dr. Robert Simons. He listened to her concerns and sat down next to her in his private office.

"I am not sure if I can give you the answers you need. Science has made great strides in the medical world, but we understand less about the mechanism of human consciousness than we do the exploration of the universe. It's difficult to explain. There are not enough studies being done to map out the realities of the conscious mind, or coma, for that matter. But there seems to be a connection. Your loss of time and reality may have been replaced by another realm of existence, a safe place until your physical self was capable of maintaining on its own, essential to fight the virus in your body. Keeping you in an unconscious state allowed your body to survive without the trauma of the battle itself. You are one of the lucky ones. I can't begin to explain what your unconscious state actually experienced."

"Doctor, I have the strange feeling that I traveled outside of my body. To another time, in another life, a completely different reality," Kathryn implored. "Did I lose my mind?"

Dr. Simons sat silently for a moment.

"I'm sorry I can't be of more comfort to you. We simply don't know enough about the unconscious mind even though consciousness is the basis for life itself."

Kathryn felt a moment of hopelessness and looked down at the floor.

The doctor took her hand in his and looked into her eyes.

"If you are willing to take a leap of faith, I do have a suggestion. I would like you to contact Sybil Rakin. She is a psychic and healer who deals with the mind, and a good one. She has helped many others with a similar dilemma. I've been told she may give you valuable insight. Her offices are in San Francisco."

When Kathryn and her sister drove to her home, they discussed the visit with Dr. Simons.

"Was the good doctor helpful, Kate?"

"Perhaps, but it isn't enough. He said I should contact a Sybil Rakin in San Francisco."

"The psychic? She's famous! Are you going to call her?"

"I think I should. I'd like to look her up on the internet when we get back, okay?"

"Sure. And I'll travel to San Francisco with you. I've always wanted to go anyway."

"Thanks, Jackie."

The next day she called Ms. Rakin's office and made an appointment for a private visit. She would see her in a few days.

Jackie made airline reservations for them as well as reservations at the Hotel Riu Plaza Fisherman's Wharf. She insisted on giving Kathryn a short holiday after her life and death experience with Covid. The Hotel Riu was on the waterfront with wonderful sites and attractions to keep them busy.

"Mommy and Aunt Jackie are going away for a couple days, Pumpkin. Uncle Matt will take good care of you. We'll bring back a special surprise for you, Okay?"

"Yes," chimed in Matt. "We're going to have lots of fun together. Maybe we'll even get a real kitty."

Melissa's eyes lit up, "Yeah, a real kitty."

"Mommy will call you everyday day, Sweetheart," said Kathryn, giving her a kiss on her forehead and a warm hug.

"Okay, Mommy."

Upon arriving in San Francisco, Kathryn and Jackie checked into the hotel and immediately went to the window to see the marvelous view of the bay and Fisherman's Wharf.

"This is beautiful," said Jackie.

As Kathryn looked down on the waterfront, an odd, déjà vu' moment came over her.

"Where are all the ships? Where are the tall ships?"

"I see one, Kate. The travel brochure says it is the Balclutha. They have tours on that ship."

Kathryn sat down by the window and looked at the ship while a melancholy feeling filled her heart.

CHAPTER 8

In the morning, they both enjoyed breakfast and set out for exploration. Kathryn's appointment with Sybil Rakin was at 3 p.m. They would play tourists until it was time to go.

Neither of them had ever been to San Francisco before. But somehow, the city seemed familiar to Kathryn, even the smells of the waterfront and the Pacific Ocean air itself. They had Shrimp Louie for Lunch at a restaurant on Pier 39, then shopped along the wharf. Kathryn bought a charming snow globe for Melissa, and afterward, they sampled Ghirardelli chocolate, followed by a tour on the Balclutha.

The instant Kathryn set foot on the legendary ship, a flashback struck her mind like a lightning bolt. She searched the faces of the others who were onboard, searching for the recognition of someone, someone she knew. But they were all strangers. A sadness welled up inside of her. Thankfully, her sister's voice brought her back to the present.

"Kate, this is a really beautiful ship. All the woodworking is meticulously carved, and the deck is spotless. Oh, and look at all the seals at the pier. Such a wonderful place."

"It is, isn't it? I'm so glad we came here together."

Kathryn smiled while taking in a deep breath of the ocean air. It was a perfect sunny day. Even so, she longingly looked past the Golden Gate Bridge and out to sea. What did it all mean?

Kathryn's appointment time with Sybil soon approached, and they hired a cab to take them to her offices. When they arrived, Jackie sat down in the lobby to wait for her. Then someone took Kathryn to see Sybil. The moment Sybil saw Kathryn, she knew exactly what had happened to her. She led her to a nearby sofa.

"My dear Kathryn, you've been on quite a journey. Bless your heart. Let's sit and talk."

"Thank you for seeing me on such a short notice, Ms. Rakin. I had a bad experience when I first came out of an induced coma due to Covid. It's okay, I'm well now. But at that time, I lost consciousness again when a nightmarish, otherworldly reality came over me. Like I was somewhere else, not myself, in places I can't remember. Yet, now they are haunting me."

Tears rolled down Kathryn's face, and Sybil handed her a tissue.

"Yes, indeed. You were someplace else. Please call me Sybil."

"Thank you, I will."

"Kathryn, you were on a journey into your past lives. It is a very rare gift to cross the space-time continuum and return to yourself again. Let me try to explain all this to you. Please stop me whenever you wish."

Sybil took her by the hand.

"When you were very sick and in a coma, your mind protected you. But the shock of returning to the present triggered past lives through retro traumatic moments in those lives."

"Sybil, you know, it's strange. When I came to San Francisco, I had the odd sensation that I'd been here before. So many things seemed so familiar, and yet, others didn't."

"And they should," continued Sybil. "You lived in San Francisco in the mid- 1800s. In fact, you had a life in Germany during World War II and again in early 1900."

Kathryn couldn't believe her ears. Yet, deep inside it all made sense.

"How far back did I go?"

"You were also a young woman in the New England 1700s."

Kathryn looked about the room, slowly digesting Sybil's information.

"Those lives ended early. You did not grow old. But this life will last long into your nineties. It will be your last incarnation on this planet, in this dimension. The Other Side, Heaven, is your true home. You will return rich with the experiences of life in the flesh."

Kathryn slowly nodded, accepting her explanation.

"My dear, the spirit, the soul, never forgets. The experiences of past lives are retained in our cell memory. Sometimes, trauma can awaken those memories, good or bad. Just remember, if a place or person seems particularly familiar to you, it is because it is, they are. You encountered that place or person in another life, another time. Trust your intuition."

Kathryn sat for a moment in silence.

"Thank you so much, Sybil. I will work on that. I'm so happy we had this talk. I feel as if a weight has been lifted already."

Sybil gently gave her a hug. Holding her hand, she said, "Bless your heart. I am here for you anytime you need me. I will notify my staff to alert me if you need to talk again."

The following day, Kathryn and Jackie flew back to Chicago. While her sister watched a movie on the flight, Kathryn sat by the window looking down at the world from 35,000 feet. She used that time of solitude to appreciate the mysteries of life and the unique intricacies of existence. In many ways, she felt wiser, more grateful than ever before. She also had a deeper appreciation for the life she was living.

Melissa and Matt met them at the door as soon as they arrived. Kathryn ran to her daughter and gave her a big hug.

"Mommy, I have a new kitty. A real kitty! Come in, Mommy. I want to show you my kitty."

Kathryn gave Matt a beautiful smile.

"Thank you for taking care of Missy for me."

Matt gave Kathryn and Jackie hugs to welcome them home.

"We had a great time."

They settled down inside, and Melissa brought her kitty to Kathryn. It was a sweet grey female, almost silver, who purred and talked to them right away.

"What a pretty kitty, Missy. What did you name her?" asked Kathryn.

"Melissa proudly said, "Her name is Gabby. I love her very much."

"Then so do I. Mommy brought you something from San Francisco, but it's not as nice as your kitty."

She handed Melissa her snow globe. Inside it was the Golden Gate Bridge.

"Thank you, Mommy. I love this too."

Melissa shook the globe and showed it to Gabby, who immediately tried to play with the floating snow.

"Was it a successful trip?" asked Matt.

Jackie answered first, "I believe it was. Plus, we had a wonderful time, didn't we, Kate?"

"Yes, we did."

Kathryn sat on the floor, playing with Melissa and Gabby.

"So, maybe we should travel again real soon. Let's go next summer. Maybe a cruise?"

"No, no," Kathryn quickly replied. "Let's fly."

"Okay, where shall we go?"

A wisp of a memory came to Kathryn's mind, and she smiled.

"Ireland."

T. L. Conn is an American author. She performed many years as a theatrical actress; and as a vocalist. She also has published work on Amazon with her book titled, "Cascades."

Intentionally Left Blank

88

Intentionally Left Blank

89

Intentionally Left Blank

Intentionally Left Blank

91

Intentionally Left Blank

92

Intentionally Left Blank

93

Intentionally Left Blank

94

Intentionally Left Blank

95

Intentionally Left Blank

96

96

* 9 7 9 8 2 1 8 1 9 2 5 2 5 *